.95

D1575675

PLAID TO THE BONE

The Time Warp Trio™ television series is produced by WGBH
in association with Soup2Nuts for Discovery Kids.

Harper Trophy® is a registered trademark of HarperCollins Publishers.

Time Warp Trio®
Time Warp Trio: Plaid to the Bone
Copyright © 2007 WGBH Educational Foundation and Chucklebait, Inc.
Artwork, Designs and Animation © 2006 WGBH Educational Foundation

For information address HarperCollins Children's Books,
a division of HarperCollins Publishers,
1350 Avenue of the Americas, New York, NY 10019.
www.harpercollinschildrens.com

Library of Congress catalog card number: 2006935096
ISBN-10: 0-06-111642-4 — ISBN-13: 978-0-06-111642-1

Book design by Joe Merkel
❖
First Harper Trophy edition, 2006

TIME WARP TRIO™

vol. 3

PLAID TO THE
B O N E

CREATED BY
JON SCIESZKA

ADAPTED BY
AMY COURT-KAEMON

ADAPTED FROM THE
TELEPLAY BY
PETER K. HIRSCH

HarperTrophy®
An Imprint of HarperCollinsPublishers

TIME WARP TRIO

CHARACTERS

JOE

JOE'S AN AVERAGE KID WITH AN INCREDIBLE BOOK. *THE BOOK* ALLOWS HIM AND HIS TWO BEST FRIENDS TO TRAVEL ACROSS ALL DIMENSIONS OF TIME AND SPACE.

JODIE

JODIE IS JOE'S GREAT-GRANDDAUGHTER. SHE IS THE NEXT IN A LONG FAMILY LINE OF MAGICIANS AND TIME TRAVELERS, AND THE RIGHTFUL OWNER OF *THE BOOK* IN 2105.

ANNA

JOE'S KID SISTER MAY BE YOUNG, BUT THERE'S NO DENYING IT—SHE IS A NATURAL-BORN WARPER WITH A KNACK FOR MAGIC. SHE'S REALLY GOOD AT SPYING ON—AND ANNOYING—HER OLDER BROTHER.

THE BOOK

JOE RECEIVED *THE BOOK* AS A BIRTHDAY PRESENT FROM HIS UNCLE JOE. IT CAN WARP ANYONE TO ANY TIME AND ANY PLACE IN HISTORY. WHILE THAT SOUNDS REALLY COOL, THERE'S ONE PROBLEM: THE ONLY WAY TO GET BACK TO WHERE YOU CAME FROM IS TO FIND *THE BOOK* IN THE TIME AND PLACE YOU WARPED INTO. AND WHENEVER *THE BOOK* IS USED FOR TIME TRAVEL, IT HAS A HABIT OF DISAPPEARING.

BLACK AGNES

ALSO KNOWN AS LADY AGNES RANDOLPH, THIS FEISTY MEDIEVAL SCOTSWOMAN FOUND HER HOME, CASTLE DUNBAR, UNDER SIEGE IN 1338. WITH HER HUSBAND, THE EARL OF MORAY, OFF FIGHTING, BLACK AGNES MAY HAVE LOOKED LIKE AN EASY TARGET TO THE ENGLISH FORCES. BUT BOY, WERE THEY WRONG!

UNCLE JOE

ONCE THE KEEPER OF *THE BOOK*, MAGICAL UNCLE JOE WAS NEVER ALL THAT GREAT AT HARNESSING ITS POWERS. BUT AFTER GIVING *THE BOOK* TO HIS NEPHEW AS A BIRTHDAY PRESENT, UNCLE JOE FINDS HIMSELF "BORROWING" IT BACK EVERY NOW AND THEN.

MAD JACK

WATCH OUT! HE'S JOE AND ANNA'S OTHER UNCLE. . . . HE'S LURKING IN THE SHADOWS TRYING TO STEAL BACK *THE BOOK* FOR EVIL PURPOSES. WHY'S HE SO MAD? IT MAY HAVE SOMETHING TO DO WITH HIS GOAL OF BECOMING "THE RULER OF ALL SPACE AND TIME."

SEEMINGLY FROM OUT OF NOWHERE . . .

POP!

YOU HELD *THE BOOK* FOR ONE SECOND AND WARPED US TO THE MIDDLE OF NOWHERE?

IT'S BECAUSE YOU PUT IT ON THAT PINBALL MACHINE! WHO KNOWS, MAYBE YOU'VE WARPED US INSIDE OF ONE!

THAT'S RIDICULOUS! WE'RE JUST IN A . . . PARK. SOMEWHERE. . . .

IF IT IS A PARK, THAT'S ONE NASTY GAME OF CAPTURE THE FLAG.

FROM DOWN THE HILL, A SOLDIER SUDDENLY SPOTS THE TRIO.

DON'T JUST STAND THERE— TAKE THIS BALL TO THE TREBUCHET, NOW!

WHAT'S A TREBUCHET?*

*A TREBUCHET IS A MEDIEVAL WEAPON.

JODIE, JOE, AND ANNA HAVE NO CHOICE BUT TO ROLL A GIANT BOULDER TOWARD THE CAMP.

UGGGH!

NGHHH!

JODIE THINKS FAST.

TO . . . THE KING?

WHICH KING? EDWARD III OR DAVID BRUCE?

WAIT A MINUTE— IT'S A TRICK QUESTION! THERE AREN'T TWO KINGS, RIGHT?

BUT THE EARL OF SALISBURY DOESN'T WANT TO HEAR IT.

SALISBURY RAISES HIS SWORD . . .

. . . AND CUTS THE ROPE.

THA-

THWIPPP

11

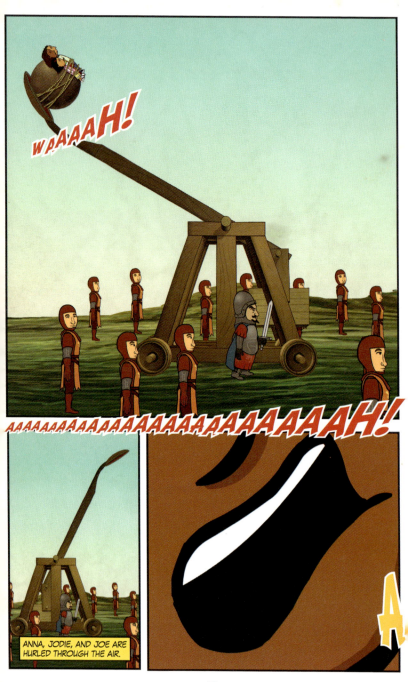

WAAAAH!

AAAAAAAAAAAAAAAAAAAAAAAAAAAAAAAAAH!

ANNA, JODIE, AND JOE ARE HURLED THROUGH THE AIR.

YEAH! SO NOW THAT WE'VE BONDED—WILL YOU TEACH ME SOMETHING ABOUT *THE BOOK*?

SEE? I TOLD YOU.

ANNA, I KNOW YOU'VE DONE IT BEFORE, BUT YOU'RE REALLY TOO YOUNG TO TIME TRAVEL. BUT, I GUESS THERE ARE ONE OR TWO LITTLE THINGS I COULD SHOW YOU.

WAIT, NO FAIR! I'M OLDER! YOU SHOULD BE TEACHING ME FIRST!

AGE DOESN'T MATTER!

DOES TOO!

DOES NOT!

IF YOU TWO DON'T STOP FIGHTING, I'M NOT SHOWING EITHER OF YOU A THING.

NOW, BEFORE YOU OPEN *THE BOOK*, YOU SHOULD ALWAYS MAKE SURE YOUR HANDS ARE CLEAN.

I USUALLY CARRY AROUND SOME DISINFECTING LOTION JUST FOR THIS PURPOSE.

WAIT— THERE'S TOMATO SAUCE ON THIS TABLE.

WE SHOULD PUT *THE BOOK* SOMEPLACE CLEAN.

Hmmm . . .

A STRANGE, GREEN GLOW COMES FROM THE PINBALL MACHINE . . .

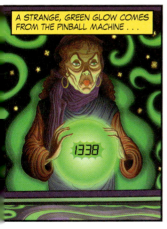

1338

"1338?" PHHT! I COULD GET THAT SCORE WITH ONE HAND TIED BEHIND MY BACK.

JUST AS JOE SETS *THE BOOK* DOWN . . .

THWINK!

. . . A STRANGE YELLOW LIGHT SURROUNDS THEM.

Zzzzzzzzzsssssssshhhh!

. . . AND THEY ARE WARPED AWAY.

pop!

18

BACK IN MEDIEVAL SCOTLAND, JODIE, JOE, AND ANNA ARE ON A COLLISION COURSE WITH . . .

AAAAAAAAAAAH!

. . . A CASTLE!

AAAAAAH!

20

INSIDE, **BLACK AGNES*** OF CASTLE DUNBAR ANXIOUSLY WAITS.

I WONDER WHAT NEW TREACHERY THAT BLACK-HEARTED EARL HAS COOKED UP FOR ME TODAY.

*LADY AGNES RANDOLPH WAS KNOWN AS BLACK AGNES BECAUSE OF HER DARK HAIR AND FEISTY SPIRIT.

AAAAAAH!

SWOOSH!

THE TRIO LANDS SAFELY ON AGNES'S BED.

WHUNK!

SENDING CHILDREN OVER THE WALL? THAT'S A NEW LOW, SALISBURY.

WITH HER SWORD, BLACK AGNES FREES THE KIDS FROM THE STONE.

YOU'RE ALRIGHT, THEN? NO BROKEN BONES? GOOD. YOU CAN LET YOURSELF OUT THROUGH THE MAIN GATE.

BUT THAT CHUBBY DUDE WITH THE GOATEE WILL KILL US!

I DEMAND TO SPEAK TO THE PERSON IN CHARGE!

WHAT THE EARL OF SALISBURY DOES WITH YA IS HIS BUSINESS.

THIS CASTLE HAS BEEN UNDER SIEGE FOR NEARLY FIVE MONTHS.

WE DON'T HAVE FOOD FOR THREE EXTRA MOUTHS!

WITH MY HUSBAND AWAY, THE ENGLISH THOUGHT WE WOULDN'T PUT UP MUCH OF A FIGHT.

YELLING AT THE SOLDIERS CAMPED OUTSIDE . . .

WELL, I GUESS YOU WERE WRONG ABOUT THAT, YOU GREEDY SWINES!

BLACK AGNES EYES THE TRIO, AND SEES SOMETHING IN ANNA THAT SHE LIKES.

CONSTABLE MACDOOHICKEY!

PUT THESE TWO IN IRONS UNTIL I DECIDE WHAT TO DO WITH THEM.

KA-KLICK!

LEAVE THE WEE ONE WITH ME. SHE'S FULL OF SPIRIT. I LIKE THAT.

GULP!

JOE AND JODIE ARE LED DEEP INTO THE CASTLE'S DUNGEON.

YOU'LL GET ONE BOWL OF OATS A DAY. ANY COMPLAINTS, AND YE CAN HAVE A STRETCH ON THE RACK INSTEAD.

THE RACK— THAT'S THE TORTURE DEVICE THAT PULLS YOUR ARMS AND LEGS OUT OF THEIR SOCKETS, RIGHT?

UH-HUH. THE OATS CAN'T BE *THAT* BAD.

JUST THEN, A FAMILIAR VOICE RINGS OUT.

YOU HAVEN'T TASTED THEM YET.

THEY'RE EXCEEDINGLY LUMPY.

UNCLE JOE!

WHAT ARE YOU DOING *HERE*?

24

OH, JUST SEEING THE SIGHTS. BUT THAT'S ALL IN THE PAST!

NOW YOU'RE HERE TO SAVE ME.

UMM, ACTUALLY, WE WERE HOPING *YOU* WERE HERE TO SAVE *US*.

BUTTERFINGERS HERE DROPPED *THE BOOK* ON A PINBALL MACHINE AND NOW WE HAVE NO IDEA WHERE IT IS.

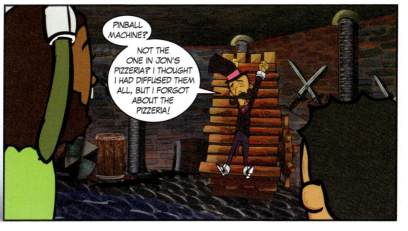

PINBALL MACHINE?

NOT THE ONE IN JON'S PIZZERIA? I THOUGHT I HAD DIFFUSED THEM ALL, BUT I FORGOT ABOUT THE PIZZERIA!

DIFFUSED *WHAT*? PINBALL MACHINES?

NO. TIME BOMBS.

THEY PROPEL UNSUSPECTING WARPERS TO A RANDOM DATE WHEN *THE BOOK* COMES IN CONTACT WITH THEM.

THEN JOE REALIZES . . .

MY SCORE! 1338!

THAT MUST BE THE YEAR WE'VE WARPED TO!

BUT WHO WOULD . . .

ZOINKS!

MAD JACK!

HE'S COMING FOR *THE BOOK.* AND FOR *YOU!* IF ONLY I COULD REACH MY POCKET. I HAVE THE PERFECT LOCK-PICKING DEVICE.

WAIT! I MAY HAVE SOMETHING IN *MY* POCKET THAT COULD HELP.

JOE, SEE IF YOU CAN REACH IT.

JUST A LITTLE BIT FARTHER! STRETCH! *STRETCH!*

ON THE PARAPET, BLACK AGNES AND ANNA WATCH AS SALISBURY AND HIS TROOPS LAUNCH THEIR LATEST ATTACK ON CASTLE DUNBAR.

COME CLOSER, SALISBURY, SO I CAN SEE YOUR *SAFT TATTIE* OF A FACE— THAT'S SCOTTISH FOR "MUSHY POTATO."

FWOOSH!

BUT SALISBURY AND HIS MEN ARE GETTING A LITTLE TOO CLOSE

BWOMF!

KA-

SMASH!

HA! BARELY NICKED US!

WHY ARE THEY ATTACKING YOU, ANYWAY?

FOR LAND. BUT WE SCOTS WON BACK OUR RIGHTS TO OWN LAND 24 YEARS AGO, AND NOW THEY HAVE NO BUSINESS HERE.

JUST THEN, THE TREBUCHET LAUNCHES ANOTHER STONE BALL AT THE CASTLE.

OH, NO!

KA-SMASH!

NOT THE LIBRARY!

LIBRARY! LADY AGNES, DID YOU HAVE A BLUE BOOK ABOUT THIS SIZE IN THERE??

Hmmm . . .

WITH SILVER SQUIGGLY THINGS ON IT?

YES! YES! THAT'S IT!

WHEN THE TRIO ARRIVED IN *MEDIEVAL SCOTLAND*, THE SCOTTISH AND THE ENGLISH WERE LOCKED IN A BATTLE OVER LAND.

BATTLE-CAM

SCOTLAND HAD BEEN INDEPENDENT, BUT IN THE EARLY 1300'S THE KING OF ENGLAND TRIED TO INSTALL HIS OWN GOVERNMENT.

IN 1314, THE SCOTTISH KING HAD A GREAT VICTORY AND *THE SCOTS* WON BACK THEIR LAND.

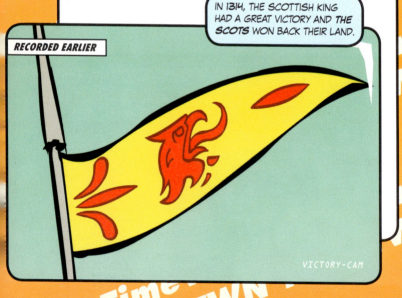

RECORDED EARLIER

VICTORY-CAM

IN THE DUNGEON . . .

NᴳGGGH!

. . . JOE STRETCHES TO REACH JODIE'S POCKET.

NOW WHAT?

SQUIRT SOME ON MY HANDS.

SQUirsh!!

JODIE SLIPS FROM HER CUFFS . . .

SCHLLP!

. . . AND FREES HERSELF.

OH YEAH!

QUICK! THE TOOL IS IN MY INSIDE POCKET!

A PEN? THIS IS THE PERFECT LOCK-PICKING DEVICE?

IT'S NOT JUST *A* PEN, MY DEAR. IT'S *THE* PEN.

BUT BEFORE JODIE CAN TEST IT OUT, IT SPRINGS FROM HER HAND LIKE IT HAS A MIND OF ITS OWN.

HEY!

BOING!

ZASH!

HEEL, PEN! HEEL!

NOW BE A GOOD PEN AND GET US OUT OF HERE.

KA-

ZAP!

PEN FLIES THROUGH THE AIR TOWARD JOE . . .

KRACK!

KA-

ZASH!

KRICK

KRACK!

WHOA!

. . . AND THEN DRAWS A QUESTION MARK IN THE AIR.

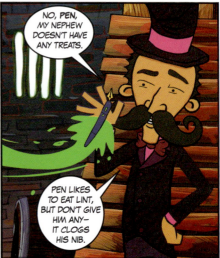

NO, PEN, MY NEPHEW DOESN'T HAVE ANY TREATS.

PEN LIKES TO EAT LINT, BUT DON'T GIVE HIM ANY— IT CLOGS HIS NIB.

UNCLE JOE GRABS PEN AND AIMS HIS NIB AT THE LOCKED DOOR.

KA-ZOOSH!

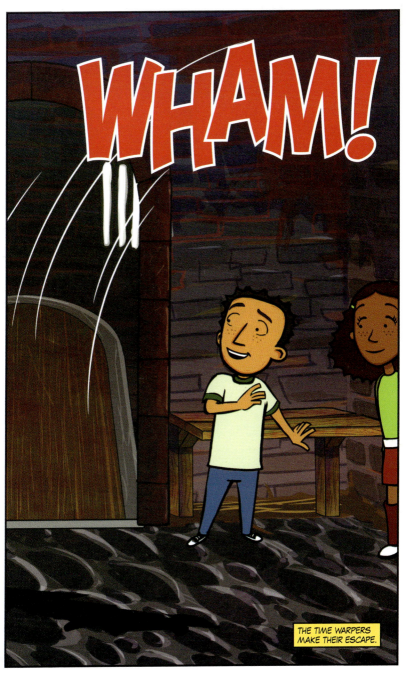

THE TIME WARPERS
MAKE THEIR ESCAPE.

ANNA AND BLACK AGNES ARE TOURING THE PARAPET . . .

. . . AND IF THEY GET PAST THE DRAWBRIDGE, WE'LL DROP THIS HEAVY WOODEN GATE— THE PORTCULLIS— ON THEM.

. . . WHEN ALL OF A SUDDEN, JOE, JODIE, AND UNCLE JOE RETURN.

YOU THREE! COME BACK HERE!

GASP!

UNCLE JOE!

ANNA IS EXCITED, BUT BLACK AGNES SPOTS SOMETHING TERRIFYING.

CONSTABLE MACDOOHICKEY! SOUND THE ALARM!

NO NEED, YOUR LADYSHIP. I'LL HAVE THESE PESKY GOATS HOBBLED IN A WEE BIT.

IT'S NOT THE PRISONERS I'M WORRIED ABOUT! THE SOW IS COMING!

NO! NOT THE SOW! ALL HANDS TO THE CASTLE WALLS!

AH, LADY AGNES! I FEAR THERE'S BEEN A MISUNDERSTANDING . . .

WE'RE NOT SPIES, WE SWEAR!

41

IT DOESN'T MAKE ANY DIFFERENCE NOW. UNLESS THERE'S A MIRACLE, THIS CASTLE WILL BE IN FLAMES IN MINUTES.

A GIANT WOOD TANK IS COMING TOWARD THE CASTLE.

FWOOSH!

FWOOSH!

FWOOSH!

ON IT ARE HIDDEN SOLDIERS SHOOTING FLAMING ARROWS!

THAT'S THE SOW? I WAS KIND OF HOPING IT WAS JUST A REALLY BIG PIG!

MAYBE THERE'S SOME BACK DOOR WE CAN ESCAPE FROM . . .

FLOING!

THE TRIO KNOWS UNCLE JOE IS RIGHT. THE BOOK CONTROLS ALL SPACE AND TIME. WITHOUT IT, HISTORY COULD BE ERASED.

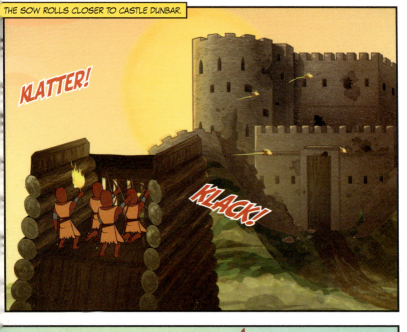

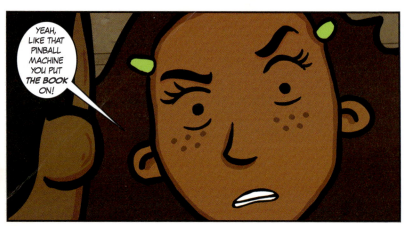

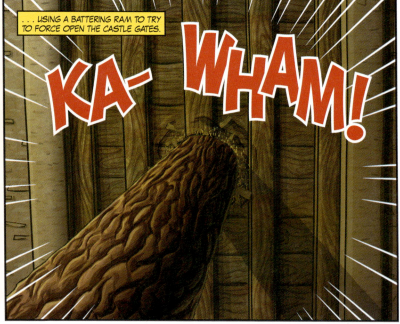

MEANWHILE . . .

A LITTLE TO THE RIGHT . . .

MORE . . .

STOP!

WE'RE READY!

OKAY! ON MY COUNT— ONE, TWO, *LIFT!*

THE GREAT STONE BALL BEGINS ROLLING DOWN THE TRACK.

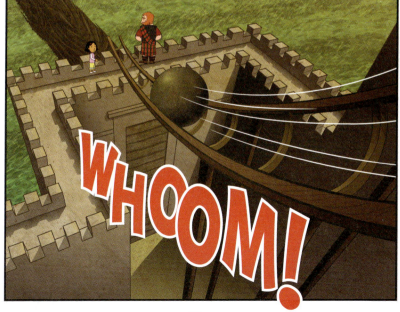

WHOOM!

NOW THAT WE'VE DEFEATED THE ENGLISH, COULD WE TAKE A LOOK AROUND THE CASTLE? THERE'S A LEGEND WE'D LIKE TO INVESTIGATE.

BUT WE DID TAN THEIR HIDES TODAY! AND TONIGHT, THERE WILL BE FEAST IN YOUR HONOR!

DEFEATED THE ENGLISH? IT WOULD TAKE MORE THAN A BIG ROCK TO DO THAT! NO, THEY'LL BE BACK TOMORROW.

Mmm . . .

THIS IS THE FEAST?

AYE. AND I GAVE YOU EACH AN EXTRA PEA, SO I DON'T WANT TO BE HEARING ANY COMPLAINTS!

WANNA TRADE TURNIPS?

NO WAY.

THIS FLY WON'T LEAVE ME ALONE! SHOO! SHOO!

BZZZZ!

BZZZZ!

I'M SORRY IT COULDN'T BE MORE, BUT WE BARELY HAVE ENOUGH TO LIVE ON.

WE ARE MOST GRATEFUL, LADY AGNES. NOW, ABOUT THIS SO-CALLED FAERIE BOOK MY NIECE WAS TELLING ME ABOUT . . .

A BREATHLESS SOLDIER BURSTS INTO THE ROOM.

I'VE JUST HEARD WORD FROM A VILLAGER—SIR RAMSAY, LORD OF DALHOUSIE, AND HIS ARMY ARE JUST EAST OF KIRKCALDY!

HE'S A FRIEND OF MY HUSBAND!

DO THEY KNOW OF OUR PLIGHT?

HE DIDN'T SAY.

JODIE SWATS AT A FLY BUZZING AROUND HER.

BZZZZ!

BZZZZ!

GET AWAY!

WITH THEIR HELP, WE COULD SEND SALISBURY PACKING ONCE AND FOR ALL! WE HAVE TO GET WORD TO THEM. . . .

ANY VOLUNTEERS?

JODIE, YOU'RE A GIRL AFTER MY OWN HEART, RISKING YOUR LIFE FOR A BUNCH OF STRANGERS— BLESS YOU!

BUT . . . BUT . . .

I THINK WHAT SHE'S TRYING TO SAY IS, PERHAPS WE SHOULD ALL GO ON THIS IMPROMPTU EXPEDITION.

DID YOU KNOW THAT MOST MEDIEVAL BATTLES WERE **NOT** FOUGHT BETWEEN KNIGHTS ON OPEN FIELDS, BUT BETWEEN **SIEGE WEAPONS** AND **CASTLES**?

FLAMING ARROWS

BATTERING RAM

THE **EARL OF SALISBURY'S** ARMORY INCLUDED A **SOW—** WHICH WAS A HUGE TANK AND BATTERING RAM. THERE WAS A PLATFORM ON TOP OF IT WHERE SOLDIERS STOOD, SHOOTING **FLAMING ARROWS**. THE **BATTERING RAM** COULD SMASH THROUGH CASTLE DOORS WITH EASE. DEFENDERS WOULD THROW THINGS OFF THE WALLS ABOVE TO TRY TO STOP IT. SOMETIMES THEY THREW **GIANT ROCKS** AND SOMETIMES THEY THREW . . . **BOILING OIL**. YIKES!

SOW-CAM

ARCHER PLATFORM

SOW-CAM

THE **TREBUCHET** WAS LIKE A **GIANT SLINGSHOT**. ONE END WAS LOADED WITH HEAVY ROCKS AND THE OTHER END WAS LOADED WITH A **BOULDER** OR **BEEHIVES**. WHEN THE CATCH WAS RELEASED, THE TREBUCHET WOULD FLING THE BOULDER (OR BEEHIVES) **HUNDREDS OF FEET** AWAY WITH DEADLY ACCURACY.

COUNTERWEIGHT OF HEAVY ROCKS

BOULDER

TREBUCHET-CAM

A **TREBUCHET** COULD HURL A **300 POUND BOULDER** AS FAR AS **300 YARDS**. THAT'S THE LENGTH OF THREE FOOTBALL FIELDS!

AND NOW BACK TO OUR STORY, ALREADY IN PROGRESS . . .

AFTER DINNER, JOE, ANNA, AND UNCLE JOE WATCH AS JODIE EMBARKS ON THE MISSION.

OH, BOY!

I HOPE SHE'LL BE ALL RIGHT.

SHE MIGHT BE SAFER OUT THERE THAN IN HERE. I CAN FEEL MAD JACK WATCHING OUR EVERY MOVE.

HOW ARE WE GOING TO GET TO *THE BOOK* BEFORE HE DOES? ALL THE LEGEND SAID WAS THAT IT WAS SOMEWHERE WITHIN THE CASTLE WALLS!

WAIT! WE *DO* HAVE ONE ADVANTAGE OVER HIM!

ALAKAZAM!

A PIECE OF PAPER APPEARS BEFORE THEM.

"ASPIRIN . . . SOY MILK . . . CAT FOOD . . ." THIS IS A *SHOPPING LIST*.

TRUE. BUT I USED IT TO MARK MY SPOT IN *THE BOOK*. AND PEN HAS AN INFALLIBLE NIB.

AFTER TAKING A LONG SNIFF OF THE SHOPPING LIST, PEN BEGINS TO TRACK *THE BOOK* BY SCENT.

HEEL, PEN! NOW GO FIND *THE BOOK*!

BACK IN THE CASTLE, JOE, ANNA, AND UNCLE JOE FOLLOW PEN'S TRAIL.

IT'S JUST A BLANK WALL. DO YOU THINK PEN SMELLED GREEN MOLD INSTEAD OF GREEN INK?

HEY, LOOK! THIS STONE IS LOOSE.

. . . AND IT TURNS INTO A SWORD OF GREEN PULSING ENERGY!

KZZAAASH!

NOT JUST MY CANE, LITTLE BROTHER. I ALSO RELY ON FOUL PLAY.

THROOSH!

MAD JACK FLINGS A HANDFUL OF MAGIC POWDER AT UNCLE JOE, RENDERING HIM HELPLESS.

HWACK!

GACK!

NO!!!

UNCLE JOE!!

JOE THROWS *THE BOOK* AT MAD JACK.

TH WOOSH!

I'M SORRY, UNCLE JOE. I JUST CAN'T DO IT. HERE. TAKE IT. IT'S YOURS.

EXCELLENT CHOICE! ALTHOUGH YOU REALLY SHOULDN'T THROW *THE BOOK.*

BUT JOE HAS A PLAN. HE REACHES FOR PEN . . .

AH-HA!

75

SOMEWHERE IN THE HIGHLANDS, JODIE AND CONSTABLE MACDOOHICKEY MAKE THEIR ESCAPE.

A-THUMP!

GA-THUMP!

I THINK WE LOST THEM!

THINK AGAIN. LOOK!

THE SILHOUETTE OF AN ARMY LOOMS BEFORE THEM.

WE'RE TRAPPED!

BUT AS THE SUN RISES . . .

BACK AT THE CASTLE, ANNA KEEPS HER HOLD ON MAD JACK.

DROP IT!

MAD JACK DROPS *THE BOOK,* AND ANNA GRABS IT.

GET OFF ME, YOU LITTLE MONSTER!

GOT IT!

YOU THINK YOU CAN WIN AGAINST ME?! YOU'VE NEVER HELD A WARP WEAPON IN YOUR LIFE!

WHEN I GET THROUGH WITH YOU, THERE'LL BE PIECES OF YOU IN EVERY ERA *SINCE THE DAWN OF TIME!*

OOOOOH!

THAT'S MY UNCLE. HE'S MAD.

I'LL SAY! THREATENING A PAIR OF WEE ONES WITH A . . . A . . . WHAT **WAS** THAT THING?

AND WHAT'S THAT IN YOUR HAND?

OH, THIS?
IT'S A . . .
UMM . . .

FLIP!

JUST
A PEN, LADY
AGNES.

THE PEN
THAT WROTE
THIS FAERIE
BOOK.

DON'T TAKE THIS THE WRONG WAY, BUT I THINK YOU'RE A FEW SHILLINGS SHORT OF A POUND.

SUDDENLY, A MESSENGER BURSTS IN.

YOUR LADYSHIP! DALHOUSIE'S MEN ARE HERE!

I HOPE JODIE'S OKAY!

QUICKLY— TO THE PARAPET!

LADY AGNES AND ANNA RUSH OFF.

WE'LL BE THERE SHORTLY. I JUST HAVE TO MAKE SURE MY BROTHER . . .

BUT **MAD JACK** IS ALREADY GONE!

BLAST IT! I SHOULD'VE TAKEN THAT POCKET WATCH FROM HIM! WELL, WE'LL JUST HAVE TO WAIT TO CATCH HIM NEXT TIME.

NEXT TIME? YOU MEAN THIS WASN'T THE BIG APOCALYPTIC SHOWDOWN THAT JODIE TOLD ME ABOUT LAST WEEK?

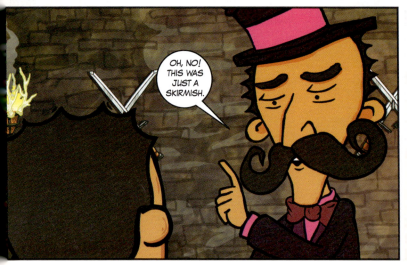

OH, NO! THIS WAS JUST A SKIRMISH.

HE ALMOST HACKED ME TO PIECES!

BUT YOU STOOD UP TO HIM. AND IF YOU USE YOUR HEAD, YOU'LL DO JUST FINE WHEN THINGS GET REALLY BAD.

COME, COME! WE MUSTN'T KEEP THE LADIES WAITING!

ON THE PARAPET, BLACK AGNES AND THE GANG WATCH AS SALISBURY AND HIS MEN RETREAT.

COME BACK ANY TIME, SALISBURY! HOPE YOU ENJOYED OUR HOSPITALITY!

IT WAS *TERRIBLE*—WE CAME THIS CLOSE TO GETTING CAUGHT, AND I GOT SICK FROM ALL THE RIDING!

SHE DIDN'T CLOSE HER MOUTH THE ENTIRE TIME! *ARE WE THERE YET? CAN WE STOP FOR A SNACK?* I THOUGHT I'D PERISH!

THEY'RE A STRANGE LOT, BUT WE OWE THEM OUR LIVES.

JODIE, FOR YOUR HELP, I AWARD YOU FIFTY OF THE FATTEST SHEEP IN THE SCOTTISH MIDLANDS!

UMM, THANKS, BUT MY BUILDING DOESN'T ALLOW PETS.

OH. WOULD YOU PREFER SOMETHING ELSE?

WE'D BE VERY GRATEFUL IF YOU ALLOWED US TO KEEP THIS FAERIE BOOK.

JOE OPENS *THE BOOK* . . .

WOOOOSH!

KZZAAASH

ZAP!

. . . AND THEY'RE WARPED AWAY.

BACK AT JON'S PIZZERIA IN BROOKLYN.

RIGHT BACK WHERE WE LEFT! HEY, YOU'RE GETTING BETTER AT. . .

WAIT A MINUTE— WHERE'S UNCLE JOE?

YOU LOST HIM!! I KNEW JODIE SHOULD HAVE WARPED US BACK!

JOE FINDS A NOTE AND A GREEN MEDAL STUCK BETWEEN *THE BOOK'S* PAGES.

HEY, WHAT'S THIS?

DEAR JOE,
SORRY TO LEAVE IN MID-WARP. I HAD SOME URGENT BUSINESS TO ATTEND TO. —UNCLE JOE.

P.S. CONGRATULATIONS ON GRADUATING TO THE NEXT LEVEL. YOU ARE NOW A TIME PAGE.

I'M A TIME PAGE! I'M A *TIME PAGE!*

JOE HAS PROVEN HIMSELF AS A TIME WARPER. HE CAN'T HELP BUT BRAG.

CHECK IT OUT! I DON'T SEE *YOU* WEARING ONE OF THESE!

THAT'S BECAUSE I HAVEN'T BEEN A TIME PAGE SINCE I WAS FIVE.

AND WITH THAT, JODIE IS GONE.

OKAY, TIME PAGE. HOW 'BOUT SOME HELP WITH MY MATH HOMEWORK?

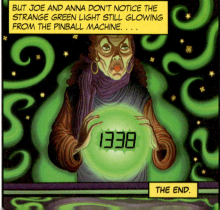

BUT JOE AND ANNA DON'T NOTICE THE STRANGE GREEN LIGHT STILL GLOWING FROM THE PINBALL MACHINE. . . .

1338

THE END.